This
Toby Story
belongs to

RUBY

For Nina and Emmett—
Gramma loves you both

LITTLE SIMON
An imprint of Simon & Schuster Children's Publishing Division
1230 Avenue of the Americas, New York, New York 10020
Copyright © 2000 by Cyndy Szekeres
All rights reserved including the right of reproduction in whole or in part in any form.
LITTLE SIMON and colophon are registered trademarks of Simon & Schuster.
Manufactured in Mexico
First Edition
2 4 6 8 10 9 7 5 3 1
ISBN 0-689-82645-1
Library of Congress Catalog Card Number 99-73499

# Toby!

by Cyndy Szekeres

LITTLE SIMON

New York    London    Toronto    Sydney    Singapore

This is Toby.

He is usually a busy little mouse.

But today when he was done playing
with his toys, he sat on his bench.

He sat and sat, and sat, and sat!

Toby was beginning to feel twitchy and itchy.
His ears wiggled and his toes began to tap.

His little pink tail went flip-flop, flip-flop.
His eyes began to wink and blink.
Toby needed something to do.

"I need to be busy!"
he complained to
his mama.

"I think it is time for your dinosaurs
to do some exercises," Mama said.

"Yes!" Toby laughed. "They can do that."

His dinosaurs
touched
the
floor.

His dinosaurs
reached for
the sky.
One, two,
three, four,
five times!

Those dinosaurs flew . . .

all around the room . . .

over and over again.

"Jump high, dinosaurs!"
called Mama.

Toby and the dinosaurs jumped.
One, two,
three, four,
five times!

"Touch the floor
        and fly once more!"
    Toby ordered.

After a lot of flying and jumping and floor touching, Toby announced,

"Now we are very strong!"

"I can hold up the world," he said.
Then he stood on his head.

"I am not upside down, I am right side
up, and I am holding up the world."

"Don't fall off, Mama!" Toby laughed.

"Come help me, my strong little mouse."

"Can you carry the picnic basket outside, under the clover?" Mama asked.

Toby did that,

and he and Mama had a lovely lunch.

"Shall we make up a dinosaur song?" Mama asked.

"Fly, fly, fly your dinosaurs,
   all around the room,"
Toby sang.

"Merrily, merrily, merrily, merrily,
don't bump into the broom!" Mama added.

"It is time for dinosaurs to nap,"
Mama told her little mouse.

Toby gathered them up
and lay his head on Mama's lap.

He held those
dinosaurs very still . . .

until they fell asleep.